AMAZING ANIMAL SELF-DEFENSE

Eye-Watering Stink
Gross Skunks

by Rex Ruby

BEARPORT
PUBLISHING

Minneapolis, Minnesota

Credits: Cover and title page, © Geoffrey Kuchera/Shutterstock, © AnnaViolet/iStock, © romiri/iStock and © Jular Seesulai/iStock; 4–5, © Tom Vezo/Minden Pictures; 7, © gkuchera/Getty Images; 8–9, © Holly Kuchera/Alamy; 10, © Adwo/Shutterstock; 10–11, © wonderful-Earth.net/Alamy; 12, © Mykyta Dolmatov/iStock; 13, © Stan Tekiela Author / Naturalist / Wildlife Photographer/Getty Images; 15, © Christian Hütter /Alamy; 16–17, © All Canada Photos/Alamy; 18–19, © agefotostock/Alamy; 20–21, © Holly Kuchera/Shutterstock; and 22, © Jouan Rius/Nature Picture Library.

Bearport Publishing Company Product Development Team
President: Jen Jenson; Director of Product Development: Spencer Brinker; Senior Editor: Allison Juda; Editor: Charly Haley; Associate Editor: Naomi Reich; Senior Designer: Colin O'Dea; Associate Designer: Elena Klinkner; Associate Designer: Kayla Eggert; Product Development Assistant: Anita Stasson

Library of Congress Cataloging-in-Publication Data

Names: Ruby, Rex, author.
Title: Eye-watering stink : gross skunks / Rex Ruby.
Description: Minneapolis, Minnesota : Bearport Publishing Company, [2023] | Series: Amazing animal self-defense | Includes bibliographical references and index.
Identifiers: LCCN 2022033663 (print) | LCCN 2022033664 (ebook) | ISBN 9798885093880 (hardcover) | ISBN 9798885095105 (paperback) | ISBN 9798885096256 (ebook)
Subjects: LCSH: Skunks--Behavior--Juvenile literature. | Animal defenses--Juvenile literature.
Classification: LCC QL737.C248 R83 2023 (print) | LCC QL737.C248 (ebook) | DDC 599.76/8--dc23/eng/20220802
LC record available at https://lccn.loc.gov/2022033663
LC ebook record available at https://lccn.loc.gov/2022033664

Copyright © 2023 Bearport Publishing Company. All rights reserved. No part of this publication may be reproduced in whole or in part, stored in any retrieval system, or transmitted in any form or by any means, electronic, mechanical, photocopying, recording, or otherwise, without written permission from the publisher.

For more information, write to Bearport Publishing, 5357 Penn Avenue South, Minneapolis, MN 55419.

CONTENTS

A Smelly Weapon 4
Under the Tail 6
Scary Skunks 8
A Warning. 10
Places to Live 12
Safe at Home. 14
Baby Skunks 16
Learning to Hunt. 18
On Their Own 20

Another Smelly Defense 22
Glossary 23
Index. 24
Read More. 24
Learn More Online 24
About the Author 24

A Smelly Weapon

It's dinnertime and a hungry fox has spotted a tasty treat. A skunk! Because the skunk can't **outrun** this enemy, the little animal should make a nice meal. Suddenly, the black-and-white animal raises its bushy tail. *Pee-yew!* A horrible smell fills the air. The fox scrambles away.

Under the Tail

Skunks spray a smelly oil called **musk** to scare off enemies. The musk is stored in two small pouches under the animal's tail. Skunks store enough musk for about six sprays at a time. The stinky oil can sting when it gets in an enemy's eyes and make them feel sick. Even worse, the bad smell can last for days!

Watch out! A skunk can spray its musk as far as 15 feet (5 m).

Scary Skunks

If an enemy gets too close, a skunk will try to scare it away before using its smelly spray. The little animal tries to look bigger by **arching** its back and lifting its tail. A skunk may also stomp its feet and hiss. If these tricks fail, the skunk bends its body into a U-shape and sprays.

A Warning

Skunks often don't need to do anything to keep enemies away a second time. Their black-and-white stripes remind **predators** that have been sprayed before not to mess with skunks again!

Great horned owls can't smell very well. They will hunt skunks even after being sprayed.

Places to Live

There are 12 kinds of skunks. North America and South America are home to 10 of them. The other two kinds of smelly sprayers live in parts of Indonesia and the Philippines. Skunks make their homes in woods, **grasslands**, deserts, or even in people's backyards.

One type of skunk scares enemies away by doing a handstand on its front paws!

SAFE AT HOME

During the day, skunks stay safe in **dens**. These homey spaces are found in hollow trees, old logs, or under buildings. Skunks can also live in underground dens. When they do, skunks often use dens other animals have left, but they can dig their own if needed.

Skunks usually live alone, but sometimes several will share a den to keep warm.

A skunk in its den

Baby Skunks

In the spring, a mother skunk gives birth in a den, too. She can have between 2 and 12 babies, or **kits**, at a time. The kits are born with their eyes closed. They are almost completely helpless and rely on their mother for food and safety.

Kits can start spraying smelly musk when they are between one and six weeks old.

Learning to Hunt

At first, kits drink only milk from their mother's body. After about six weeks, the mother skunk shows them how to find other food. The kits learn to hunt **insects**, lizards, and other small animals. They also eat fruit, leaves, and bird eggs. Skunks have a sharp sense of smell to help them sniff out food.

ON THEIR OWN

By fall, the young skunks are ready to live on their own. The little animals have learned how to hunt, find dens, and take care of themselves. And if the skunks meet any hungry foxes looking for a meal, they will be ready with a smelly trick!

Skunks in the wild live for about three years. In zoos, they can live for up to 12 years.

ANOTHER SMELLY DEFENSE

FULMAR

Skunks aren't the only animals that use a very stinky defense. The fulmar is a seabird that spits smelly oil at its enemies! The **disgusting** oil sticks to the other animals' feathers or fur. It's so sticky that the enemies might struggle to move or fly away.

A fulmar spitting its oil

GLOSSARY

arching curving

dens homes where animals can rest, hide from enemies, and have babies

disgusting very unpleasant

grasslands dry areas covered with grass where few bushes and trees grow

insects small animals with bodies that have three parts

kits baby skunks

musk an oil that has a strong smell

outrun run faster or longer than someone or something else

predators animals that hunt other animals for food

INDEX

dens 14–16
enemies 4, 6, 8, 10, 13, 22
food 16, 18
fulmar 22
fur 22
great horned owls 11
hunt 11, 18–20
kits 16–18
musk 6, 8, 17
scare 8, 13
spray 5–6, 8, 10–11, 17
stripes 10
tail 4, 6, 8

READ MORE

Klatte, Kathleen A. *Skunks at Night (Up All Night! Nocturnal Animals).* New York: PowerKids Press, 2021.

Lombardo, Jennifer. *Skunks in the Forest (Forest Creatures).* New York: Gareth Stevens Publishing, 2023.

Lundgren, Julie K. *Gross and Disgusting Smells (Gross and Disgusting Things).* New York: Crabtree Publishing, 2022.

LEARN MORE ONLINE

1. Go to www.factsurfer.com or scan the QR code below.
2. Enter "**Eye-Watering Stink**" into the search box.
3. Click on the cover of this book to see a list of websites.

ABOUT THE AUTHOR

Rex Ruby lives in Minnesota with his family. He has yet to encounter a skunk in person and hopes to keep it that way.